I0547440

THE YOUNG DETECTIVES

The Case Of The Thirteen Gold Coins

Jerry Gomez Shor Jr.

The Young Detectives – The Case of the Thirteen Gold Coins
All rights reserved
© 2017, Jerry Gomez Shor Jr.
© 2017, Artwork, Jerry Gomez Shor Jr. & Camila Quevedo
© 2017, Cover Camila Quevedo
Pukiyari Publishers

ISBN-10: 1-63065-066-8
ISBN-13: 978-1-63065-066-7

PUKIYARI PUBLISHERS
www.pukiyari.com

Dedication

I wrote these detective stories some years ago, inspired by the classic novels of Sherlock Holmes by Sir Arthur Conan Doyle, Herlock Sholmes Vs Arsenio Lupine by Maurice Leblanc and Agatha Christie's Detective Poirot, which helped me create Latino-style detectives.

English people have their style, French people have a different one, and we Latinos have our own idiosyncrasies in our way of acting and being. Ayesha and Schariar, the young detectives, are those detectives who with Latino mischief successfully unravel criminal cases, and who, without violating the law, mock it successfully and wittily.

I dedicate this first book of a series to all lovers of true justice, justice that is always in our hearts but sometimes not seen.

Every case came to my office in a mysterious way and in the form of manuscripts left under my door.

Prologue

The Young Detectives books, which will be published as separate episodes, have as their main characters the computer science students, and best friends, Schariar and Ayesha, who by one gigantic coincidence end up being involved in a police case that follows a criminal gang dedicated to extorting and stealing from business owners and other important people in different countries.

Schariar is a good-looking young man. He is white and his eyes are brown. He has a deep gaze. It only takes one conversation for him to understand anything since he's very analytical. He practices martial arts, likes to discover and study ancient cultures, and is an innate detective, to the point that he became friends with local police officers with the idea of being able to collaborate, according to him, with the investigation of certain cases.

His father is Arab, but he never professed the Muslim religion. Indeed, he rejects it as antiquated and plagued by "macho" philosophies. His mother is French, of typical Parisian family and deeply Catholic, considers the other religions as mere sects for the sole purpose of taking advantage of the human race; she does not like violence, or racial discrimination, does not believe in chosen races, and considers all human beings to be of one race.

His friend, Ayesha, is Peruvian, but of English father and mother who do not belong to any religion, although they believe deeply in God. Her parents are lovers of the occult sciences, as were most of their ancestors, to the point that they would say that in 1760 one of their ancestors, seventeen generations ago, died at the stake, accused by the Holy Inquisition of performing spells and sharing prophecies. For centuries Ayesha's family has practiced alchemy and it is said that their knowledge is so deep that they even managed to uncover the secrets of the philosopher's stone, and many more other things that I am not here to write.

Despite belonging to families so distant in lifestyle and ways of thinking, **Ayesha and Schariar** are great friends and profess to each other great affection. Together they will be involved in difficult to solve cases.

Now, for your satisfaction dear reader, I am pleased to present to you in various books every case that came to my office in a mysterious way and in the form of manuscripts left under my door by third parties; it is at their request that I reserve the right to keep their names anonymous.

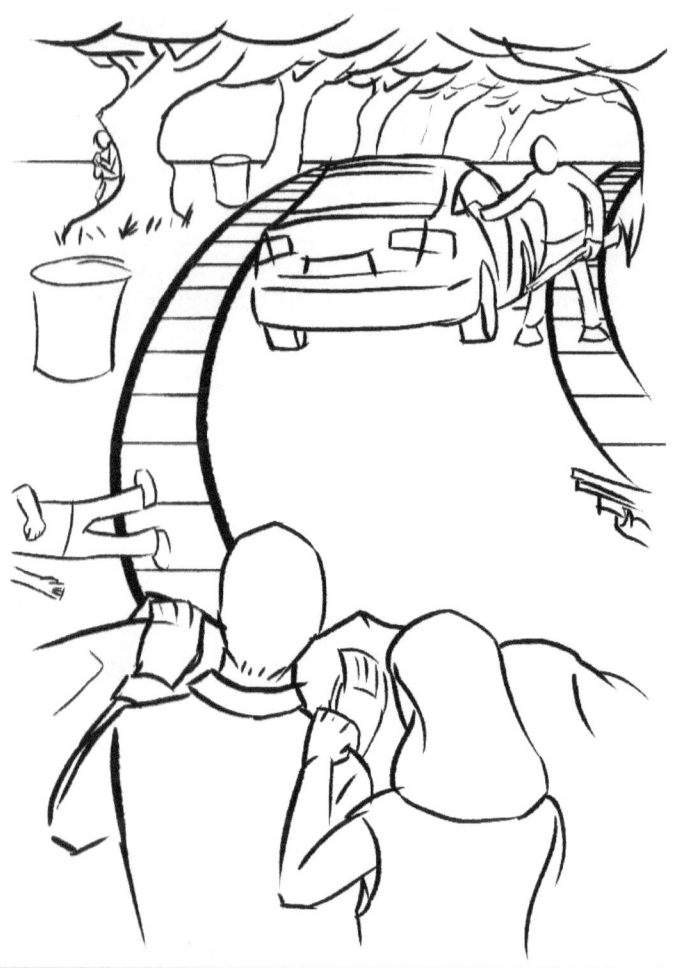

As he was about to raise the gun toward him one of his companions pulled him into the van so they could flee. At that moment Schariar read the license plate: PQ-4560, and then fainted.

An Intense Encounter

Schariar was leaving San Marcos's University campus with his inseparable friend Ayesha, after spending hours in the computer lab trying to solve a problem, when he proposed her to go to a nearby restaurant and have coffee and a sandwich. She accepted and they started walking to a coffee shop that was about three blocks from them. The street they needed to cross was always overcrowded with people and such dense traffic that cars formed bottlenecks at many points, which that day ultimately delayed them from making it to their destination by several minutes, which placed them at the exact moment and at the exact location where they would meet their fate.

All of a sudden they heard gunshots and saw a large group of people running toward the corner where they were standing. At the moment they only managed to throw themselves on the sidewalk and take shelter behind boxes that traveling merchants had left everywhere. The bullets whistled above their heads and they realized that they were, unluckily, in the midst of a shoot-out between a group of thieves and the private police of a bank a block away. Schariar himself was trembling with fear, but still he raised his head to look better from behind the boxes, and he saw six individuals covered with ski masks. He automatically thought it was a terrorist group and begged the Lord to stop the criminals from firing at them. Just then one of them saw him and stared at him and as he was about to raise the gun toward him one of his companions pulled him into the van so they could flee. At that moment Schariar read the license plate: PQ-4560, and then fainted.

I'm not sure how long he was unconscious, but when he came to he was laying on a temporary stretcher in the ambulance and, as the doctor told him, he only had a scratch in his left ear.

"Well, that's lucky! I miraculously saved my life because when the bullet grazed my ear the sound emitted by the projectile near my ear affected my brain to such an extent that it made me immediately faint and my body moved from the danger zone," said Schariar when analyzing the event from his bed in the emergency room.

They left the hospital two hours later. Ayesha accompanied him to his apartment at Avenida Pardo 345, department 201, and stayed to serve as his nurse.

Schariar clarified that he felt better and she could go home, but Ayesha insisted on staying to help him recover starting by staying the night. Her father flatly refused to let her do that, but once she explained what happened that day, he relented, although not before screaming at her over the events that led to them being in danger earlier. Ayesha always had a very close friendship with Schariar but never until that time had she stayed all night with him.

Following the doctor's advice, who explained that she had to feed him very well to compensate for the loss of blood, Ayesha went to the grocery store to buy eggs, bacon, milk and bread. When she returned, she prepared an exquisite dinner that they ate together in the bedroom, watching TV while they talked about what had happened that day.

She told him that after the shooting she had been very frightened and begged for help, because when she looked at him lying on the floor and blood running on the left side of his face she thought he had died or was close to it. And when she found out that it was only a scratch she cried with joy. They spent the whole night talking about the event until they fell asleep.

The next day they got up around noon, ate breakfast, and prepared to get going. He, to deliver a finished project to a company; and Ayesha, to go back home.

Everything went normal and without any setbacks during the following five days; but much changed from that point on...

It was probably close to five in the afternoon on Monday, January 20, when Ayesha and Schariar walked quietly down the 18th block of Avenida Brasil and when they went around the corner on to Avenida Bolívar, they were stunned by what they saw: in front of them; some fifteen meters away, was the same brown Chevrolet 67 truck that the thieves used as their getaway car. They confirmed it when they read the plate and it was then they realized that they were on that gang's territory. Schariar was the first to realize it and when he told Ayesha at first she didn't believe him, but after a moment of reflection, she replied:

"What should we do? Call the police?"

At first Schariar thought that calling the police was the right thing to do but something inside him kept bugging him to keep quiet. He knew Ayesha was waiting for his answer, so half jokingly he replied:

"Or we can investigate this case!"

To his dismay, Ayesha said, "That's not a bad idea!"

With that resolve they decided to sneak up to where the van was. They didn't see anyone inside, but they had no doubt that their hiding place would have to be the house that was right there in front of them, where a leafy tree shaded the door. They analyzed it this way: if the criminals had entered to commit any crime in that house, someone would have remained to guard the vehicle, prepared to flee. So, they approached the house, pushed the door gently, and realized that, to their great fortune, it was unlocked.

After first making sure that the entrance hall was empty of people, they crept in, hiding behind some large and heavy trunks, filled with documents and old newspapers, arranged next to a door that led to another room where the gang members were talking. What they heard next seemed to be a plan they were about to execute, they didn't understand it very well, but it gave them the impression that it was a robbery, since they mentioned something regarding thirteen gold coins, but even with that clue they were just as confused as before.

All they could think at that point was that they were unwittingly getting involved in the crime.

After a while the men decided to leave. They went away for a few hours and were not back until about 8:30 at night. They heard the door open and saw seven people enter. What surprised them most was the presence of a girl named Betty, blonde and quite attractive.

Suddenly, one of them, a fat man named Edward, stopped and asked:

"Hey Smith, didn't we left the door closed after we came in?"

"Don't be so paranoid. Nobody knows us in this country and who would want to break into an old house? Besides, if anybody would have done such a thing, our buddy Javier would've noticed," Smith replied.

As they glanced sideways, they realized that when Javier's name was mentioned the tall and sturdy young man winked at Edward, to which he responded by turning around and walking out the room closing the door behind him.

The students stayed a little longer hiding behind the trunks, until they made sure they saw them getting in the car and leaving.

They hesitated for a moment about what to do, but then decided to leave their hiding place right after Ayesha said:

"Hey Schariar, look, there's a news clipping here, and it shows an exhibition of jewels, but there is no address or the name of the hotel where this will happen... do you think it could help us?"

"It might! Save the clipping just in case!" he exclaimed.

After looking out the window and making sure they had left, they had exactly two hours at their disposal to find something in the adjoining room before leaving. Without making the slightest noise, the two friends entered the place where the outlaws had been a few moments before. The room was about four square meters, and as its only furniture it had a lamp hanging from the ceiling, a large rectangular table with seven chairs and a wooden shelf. They settled in one of those chairs and began to check the items on the table.

They found three pencils, some rulers and compasses, locksmith tools, and a map of the district of Miraflores showing a red dot between the 28 de Julio and Larco avenues. Thank God, the young man was always carrying a portable camera; so he decided to take a few photos of the map and also of the thirteen gold coins perfectly arranged so that they drew an "S", even though they had no idea what it could mean. Ayesha found a 45-gauge pistol, a steel dagger, and locksmith tools on one of the shelves, and they also took several photos of those as well.

Without noticing they spent nearly two hours looking at the different things they found at the hideout, so they had only fifteen minutes left before Don Smith and his gang returned.

They were ready to get going when they spotted a James Bond style black leather case. Upon lifting it they realized that it contained something heavy inside. They wanted to open it, but it was impossible, they stared at it while they determined what to do with it.

"Should we take it or leave it?" Ayesha asked.

They weren't sure what to do but realized that maybe those criminals were hatching a plan for something bad and since they were already involved with whatever that was they decided to take it and later look for clues inside the briefcase.

They were very excited about everything that was going on, and Ayesha exclaimed, "We are going all the way. We catch them or they catch us."

But when they went to open the door they realized it was secured with a deadbolt and padlock. They assumed the criminals did it before they left so that nobody would enter their hideout and find out something only they should know.

Turns out that even with all that security two inexperienced young adults were riffling through their secret stuff. They laughed at once and decided to leave a note for their future contender, Smith, with a letter that went like this:

Dear Mr.Smith:

We are pleased to have met you and to know about your plan that we will call "The Thirteen Gold Coins." We hope you can accomplish this. But beware that we will ruin everything, we love to hurt plans. Ah! Send our most affectionate greetings to Edward, Javier, the gorgeous Miss Betty, Juan, who you will need to fix the lock, Carlos and Gregory Bünge.

You will see us again. We almost forgot! We borrow your briefcase.

Hugs and best wishes to all.

Sincerely,
The Young Detectives

They were greatly surprised when they saw it was filled with hundred-dollar bills. They calculated that there must have been more than a million there. In addition, in one of the secret pockets of the briefcase, they found a letter addressed to Smith.

They read the letter and could not help but smile at the thought of how Mr. Smith had been discovered by some rookie wanna-be detectives. They left the letter on the table and decided to escape through a small window that led to a completely dark alley; but first, they did a good job at closing it so nobody could suspect how they had left. They had to walk close and holding hands, otherwise they would not have come together at the exit after going through a long and dark alley before they could see the street at about eighty meters from them. To their surprise, they had crossed an underground tunnel. They had to leap to grasp one of the grates facing the street opposite to where they entered, and it took them some difficulty to get out of it. They were lucky the public road was deserted. Once outside, they marked the exact address of that exit to return another day out there and give them another surprise.

They hailed a taxi and went back to the apartment. Once there, they took a shower with hot water and then placed some tools on the table to try to open the briefcase.

Seeing that they couldn't do it, they had no choice but to break the lock. It was filled with hundred-dollar bills. They calculated that there must have been more than a million there. In addition, in one of the secret pockets of the briefcase, they found a letter addressed to Smith. When they saw it, they were amazed and did not know what to do, they thought about giving it to the police, but then they decided against that, and instead they chose to open the envelope and read the note.

January 19th
Milan - Italy
Dear Mr.Smith,

My dear friend, you'll be pleased to find in this brief-case what belongs to you for the job we did two years ago, you remember, the one we called "Eleven gold coins." Good luck and greetings to all: Betty, Javier, Carlos, Edward and Gregory.

Best regards,
Mario Cassimiro

In reading the letter Schariar recalled Mario Cassimiro's name: he was one of the greatest leaders of the Italian mafia in recent memory; with connections to the Mexican and Colombian drug cartels, wanted by Interpol, and for whom a reward of one million dollars was offered. They were excited and didn't know what to do. They had a letter from Mario Cassimiro himself with his current address. If they only gave that to the police, in the condition of remaining anonymous, and the police caught Cassimiro they could claim the reward and keep the briefcase.

They thought about it a lot, deciding to continue the investigation in anonymity, and to keep that information for themselves as they figured that perhaps it could serve as a secret weapon for later. They saw in their novice detectives heads the possibility of catching Smith's whole band of thieves, perhaps even his buddy

Mario Cassimiro easily; a grave error that they would later realize. Nevertheless, they continued to investigate with more caution, as they were facing a rival much stronger than they imagined.

When they finished talking about it, they placed the letter inside the briefcase, closed it, and place it in a closet in Schariar's bedroom. After doing that, they fell asleep until the next day.

The Escape

Needless to say, from the day Schariar was wounded in the ear and Ayesha accompanied him to his apartment, her parents happily let her stay with him. Although the young adults had known each other for a long time, their parents did not trust their friendship as much, simply because they belonged to totally opposite families. They were profound scholars of the occult sciences and his parents were orthodox Catholics, so there was a fairly distant stretch between the two families. And yet what existed between Ayesha and Schariar was an exception, they considered themselves as brother and sister.

It is fair to imagine that their neighbors looked at them with suspicion, possibly thinking that the fact that two unmarried young people living together in an apartment, with Ayesha coming and going as she pleased, was not appropriate. But little by little their bad sentiments were addressed, and with the help of Ayesha and Schariar they realized that they were nothing but good friends and even came to congratulate them because of the respect they had for each other above all things, even though they both were very attractive people.

Let's now leave Schariar and Ayesha and talk about what happened at the Avenida Bolívar house after the young detectives left that mysterious note to the boss.

Smith and the gang members arrived at the house at 8:35 pm, and after entering the first room they agreed to meet again the next day in the morning. John and Edward said good-bye to Smith, and left to rest in some hidden room among those dim alleys and foul odors in La Victoria district. Javier, Carlos and Gregory decided to go for a walk through Miraflores and have a few beers until dawn.

Smith stayed home with the beautiful young Betty to relax a bit at a place that probably was in some hidden corner of the district of Jesus Maria. Before leaving to board the truck, he entered the adjoining room to pick up the briefcase, the gun and his coat. You can imagine the surprise he had when he went in and did not find the briefcase. He stopped in the middle of the room and started thinking that possibly one of his crewmembers had betrayed him, when suddenly he saw a letter addressed to him on the table; and when he read it he understood he had been discovered by two young rookie detectives. Rather than being upset, Smith was amused and even smiled a little. Smith, a white, blue-eyed man with penetrating gaze and a strong will, was one of those special people whom life's circumstances taught him to maintain patience and serenity even when encountering hard events.

Smith put the letter in his pocket, sat down on one of the chairs, and was deeply in thought for a few minutes. Then, as if nothing had happened, he said goodbye.

"Boys: we'll meet again tomorrow, congratulations!"

Smith left closing the door behind him, but as he got into the van Betty stared at him as she said, "Why did you take so long to get your coat? Did something happened? You seem disturbed by something…"

"It's nothing," Smith replied with a smile and started the truck.

As he drove the car, Smith kept thinking of the youngsters who had taken the briefcase, it was almost certain that they did not belong to any private company of detectives nor worked for any police corps; but what was most intriguing to him was that they could have warned the police where the gang members were meeting and at what time but they did not… and instead they left a letter… and with such a message. Undoubtedly, they were challenging him, but it was clear that they were newbies because they did not realize what kind of people they were dealing with. And yet they had mocked them very well without leaving the slightest trace of how they entered or how they left without Smith's spies noticing anything.

I am Smith Cross, leader of the most feared criminal band in South America, dedicated to extorting, murdering and robbing the most important people in the country... And these young people have so easily fooled our security, he thought to himself.

He started to feel some sort of respect towards those youngsters.

Schariar woke up quite early that day, went to the

kitchen to prepare some food and had breakfast with Ayesha. When they were done eating they both began to wonder about what they should do about the situation they were involved in. Suddenly, she interrupted him and said, "Let's hurry up and finish breakfast so that we can go back to the house in Avenida Bolívar and investigate some more, but this time let's make a plan and that way we won't fail. Let's go and I'll tell you what I'm thinking on our way there."

Meanwhile, at the house on Avenida Bolívar, Smith was meeting very early with all the members of his crew. It was about 7:00 in the morning, when suddenly they heard a knock on the door, everyone jumped. Comrade Javier Lamp rose quickly from his seat and with a pistol in his hand went to open it, while everyone prepared in case it was an ambush. They were armed to the teeth; after receiving such a letter signed by the young detectives, the men were nervous and tense.

Javier slowly opened the door and when he realized who was knocking, all the tensed muscles in his body relaxed. The one that had alarmed them so much was an old lady offering for sale all kinds of plastic products. She was pushing a tricycle. He quickly sent her on her way, closed the door and went back to the room where the crew was waiting, and gave them the good news. Instantly there was a sigh of relief for the gang. During the previous seconds of tense expectation, many had even held their breath, but after listening to Javier most were smiling about it.

Javier slowly opened the door and when he realized who was knocking, all the tensed muscles in his body relaxed. The one that had alarmed them so much was an old lady offering for sale all kinds of plastic products. She was pushing a tricycle.

But Smith doubted she was only a humble old woman, or if she was, he thought she had knocked on the door for better reasons than a simple sale of plastic washbowls. He thought it was likely to be a trick of the young detectives, but he kept quiet and preferred not to say anything in order not to disturb his men more than they already were.

They continued to chat and plan the great robbery. After half an hour, they decided it was time to leave the house; because it had been discovered by some young people their hide-out was no longer safe. They were about to leave through the front door when they decided it would be better to go out the back window that led to the alley and from there to the street. Once they were out, they took a taxi and hurried to their new refuge. Then they would later figure out how to pick up the truck they were leaving behind.

Meanwhile, Schariar and Ayesha had just paid twenty soles to the old woman who sold plastic stuff in exchange for information about the people in the house. The old woman told them that a tall and muscular young man quickly got rid of her.

"I don't think they suspected you at all, Granny!" said the young man, as he thought to himself, *So we continue to lead!*

They said goodbye to the old woman and prepared to execute the next stage of Ayesha's plan. Before they came they had bought in a sports shop two radio transmitters and binoculars. They decided that Ayesha would stand on the corner, by the newsstand, pretending to read the one, while watching the front door; and that if she saw any movement from the crewmembers, she would let Schariar know. Meanwhile, he would be located at the back of the street, pretending to be a pedestrian waiting for the bus. For this they were both disguised: Schariar was dressed with a blue coat, mustache and false beard, and wore a hat; Ayesha had dark glasses, her hair tied in a ponytail, and large false eyelashes. Their disguises were so brilliant that not even their parents would've recognized them at first sight.

After thirty minutes of waiting, and as Schariar was getting impatient, he observed, about sixty meters from the opposite sidewalk, that the seven members of the gang scurried through the gap where they had escaped the night before. Immediately he contacted Ayesha and asked her to get in a taxi and pick him up so they could follow Smith and his men.

Just as Smith and his men were leaving, Ayesha arrived with the driver. Schariar got in the car and they started following the group, but keeping a distance of one hundred to one hundred and fifty meters; and each time they traveled about ten blocks, they got out of the taxi and took another one, that way they managed to follow them without making them suspicious that they were being stalked and thus were able to discover their new hiding place.

They saw them enter a local with rolling metal doors, located in the district of La Molina, close to the Universidad Agraria. They wrote down the address and immediately returned to Avenida Bolívar, they even paid double fare to the taxi driver on the condition of arriving to their destination in half the time that it would normally be done. Once they got to the first hideout they went inside the house to go through everything in less than five minutes. They only found one pencil and three cigars, but since they abstained from these things, they did not even touch them. All they did next was to leave a note to Smith. Then they left as fast as they could, hopped in a taxi waiting for them at the door, and traveled along several streets, sometimes turning to the right and others to the left.

After paying the driver, they got out of the car, crossed to the other street through a narrow passage and immediately took another taxi, heading for Miraflores to collect the photos they had sent to develop; among them, the enlarged map photo. Once back in the apartment they would try to link and weave all the evidence they had obtained.

For the next two hours they went through everything they had and they came to the conclusion that they had a large number of links but that apparently none of them fit with the other.

Here's what they had:

1. Thirteen gold coins, forming an "S."

2. A map of the district of Miraflores, with a red circle between July 28 and Larco.

3. A briefcase with the content of a million and a half dollars.

4. A letter from Mario Cassimiro, in which he reminded Smith that two years ago they carried out a plan called "The Eleven Gold Coins."

5. A piece of *El Comercio* newspaper clipping, dated January 9, signaling an exhibition of world jewels in a hotel in the department of Lima without address or date of the event.

6. The new address of Smith's hideout.

7. Details of the car of the band, a brown 67 Chevrolet pickup truck, with plate PQ-4560.

It seemed to them that none of those details had anything in common with the others and were confused for a long time, until suddenly Ayesha exclaimed, "I have it, Schariar! Look at the map again, look closer, and you can see that there's a faint mark, maybe done with a pencil, it's a line that starts at July 28, enters by Larco and folds down a smaller street, one whose name is hard to see, and that forms a perfect "S.""

They had found a detail, at least they thought so, but it was still a question of what the route was. After a moment of thinking, and when, by chance, Schriar's eyes fell on the newspaper clipping, he discovered that there are several four and five-star hotels in that area, so it was very likely that one of them would be holding the jewels exhibit. Until that moment they had discovered something, but there were other clues they needed: the date and direction of the exhibit, and also the meaning of the thirteen coins forming an "S." There was no doubt that it was going to be a great robbery, the problem now was to find out at which hotel in that area would be the expo. They kept thinking and wondering what new plan they had to come up with in order to find what they were looking for, when they were overwhelmed by sleep and dozed off on the table.

Meanwhile, Smith and his crew set up in their new hideout in La Molina, said goodnight to each other and took off on different directions.

Upon arriving at the house at Av. Bolívar, the first thing he observed was a written paper addressed to him. Smith already had a good idea who had written it and that was cause to worry him a little more.

Smith, Betty and Javier Lamp took a taxi and headed straight for Avenida Bolívar, to pick up the van and find out what had happened in the house after they left.

"Javier! Did you see a car following us to La Molina?" Smith asked.

"No, sir! I don't think they are aware that we won't be returning to Avenida Bolívar."

"May God hear you!" murmured Smith, "I have a bad feeling about those nosy boys. Despite being new investigators, they are smarter than the police."

Upon arriving at the house at Avenida Bolívar, the first thing he observed was a written paper addressed to him. Smith already had a good idea who had written it and that was cause to worry him a little more. He picked it up and read it:

January 29
Dear Mr. Smith,

We wanted to say hello to you and we are very sorry that you couldn't find us earlier. We wish you good luck. Ah! We forgot to tell you that the briefcase contained a lot of money for a man like you, so we decided to take one hundred thousand dollars, and the rest we'll give it back to you on January 31. You will find it in the highest part of the first palm tree on Armendariz Street, you can go pick it up at 4 or 5 in the morning. It's an excellent time, so nobody will see it's there; thus, is not in danger of getting lost.

Best regards,
The Young Detectives

When Smith read the letter he was irritated and became even more indignant when he communicated with Fabian, the new member of the band of seven.

"Chief! I can inform you that at about 1:15 p.m. two people entered the house. One of them was a young man with a mustache, of white complexion, with black hat and measured about 1.78 meters. The other was a girl of about 24 years old, white, long eyelashes and about 1.74 meters in height. They were in here for about five minutes, at the most, and they left."

When Smith heard this, he pounced at him, shouting, "And you didn't go after them?"

"I did, boss, but after chasing them through several streets and going right and left I got lost. I swear, boss! These guys are smarter than you can imagine."

Smith was furious, grabbing him he shouted, "Idiot! For this incompetence I pay! And they say you're the best! Well, be warned, if you do not find these insolent rogues, you will be the perfect food for my pets."

Smith was a lover of marine animals, especially of those hungry animals living in distant places far from civilization, where modern man has hardly explored, fish that evoke death just by mentioning their name, those beings simply called piranha. In his clandestine residence in the city of Iquitos, he had an immense aquarium full of these abominable beings whom he fed with wild animals, and sometimes with human beings who had betrayed him.

When Fabian heard his boss' threat to pay failure with his own skin, he turned and walked to the front door. At that moment he heard a cry, "Wait, Fabian!" It was Smith, who gave him a new, more specific order, "I want them alive! Do you understand? Not a scratch. You'll see to it."

Fabian was even more irritated, but did not want to tell his boss, so he left.

Smith was in a bad mood, and did not let anyone, not even Betty, get close nor reassure him. Smith stared at a picture of the infinite sea, painted by some unknown artist, when he suddenly turned his face to the right, where Javier and Betty were, and stared at them with that eagle-like glance. When they could not stand his intense glare, they lowered their faces to the ground adopting a pensive stance.

Then Smith exclaimed, "It's not possible, the jewel exhibit will take place within twelve days, exactly on February 8, and some young rogues want to ruin the plan. I, Smith, who have done twelve acts, among them robberies and kidnappings, have never felt so cornered. As a matter of fact, the police never knew my real name and these punks are putting me in such a predicament. It's not possible! However, I long to meet them face to face. Because they are inspiring such respect in me, they are more than policemen and are about to enter my list of relevant people. But they will not be able to stop me, I swear it by my name!"

At that moment Smith lowered his arms and quietly left the house to which they would never return. The three of them got into the truck with all the things they picked up and left, making sure no one was following.

Fabian, on the other hand, went to meet some old classmates of his, to ask for help and to be able to find the enigmatic whereabouts of the unknown young people. He managed to convince ten companions and with their help began the search.

The next day, Schariar woke up feeling uneasy, and seeing that they had fallen asleep on the table, he woke Ayesha up by saying, "I don't know why, but I feel a little uneasy. Like someone is hunting us."

Ayesha, being the gentle and intelligent woman she was, answered that he was undoubtedly right to feel edgy, and that Smith would probably be exasperated at that moment by all that had happened to them, and he would surely have arranged a plan for their capture.

Schariar answered, "Yeah, you're right! Let's put this away for now and prepare our next plan. In the first place, I have a way to give him back the money, but not exactly as we had written in the letter to Smith, on top of the palm tree. We'll just write the address where he's going to pick it up, he'll find that letter at the top of that tree, so Smith's henchmen won't see us, because they're almost sure to be watching over anyone approaching that tree. Now, how do you get a paper on top of a palm tree? It is very simple my dear friend: have you ever seen those street kids who are experts in flying paper airplanes?

"Yes. What are you thinking about?" Ayesha replied.

"We will find the most expert of the boys and we will give them some twenty soles so that, along with another friend, they go walking and throwing the little paper airplane containing the location of the briefcase and when they arrive at that particular palm tree, throw the airplane in such a way that it lands in its branches. Then, pretending sadness over the loss of the toy, move on to other things. That way, the person who is watching will not suspect a thing. Now, the second thing we need to figure out is how do we find out the address of the hotel and date of the exhibition. I'll tell you what I think we should do, and if you find any problem with my idea feel free to provide suggestions. I think we should get in contact with some touristic organization, and through them we'll hold a meeting, inviting the main people in charge of each hotel in Miraflores. I propose that it should be the Asociación de Hoteles, Restaurantes y Afines, or AHORA for short."

At that moment Ayesha interrupted him saying that it would be better to connect with the tourism educational entity in the national arena known as CENFOTUR, or Centro de Formación en Turismo, a tourism training center, explaining that this institution has relations with all hotels, restaurants and travel agencies of Peru and abroad. Schariar thought it was an excellent idea, because through this organization they would be able to communicate with the person responsible for the hotel they were looking for.

After they agreed on what they needed to do, they left the house to execute the first plan to develop that day, then toured all Miraflores in search of CENFOTUR, until they found the premises of the institute three or four blocks from the famous drop of Armendariz and towards the cliff of Barranco.

When they arrived they noticed that the institute was located in an old house that had been remodeled and looked splendid. As they entered through the front door they found a large number of students with notebooks in hand. Schariar approached a group of girls who were talking in the courtyard and after greeting them he asked them about the person in charge of the institution.

One of the girls talking, the most alert and flirtatious, approached them, and winking at Schariar responded that that person was the general manager, Fernando Gomez López. And without asking Schariar the girl went on, "My name is Laurence Inchaustegui, and you?" "My name is Schariar," he replied, "and I am very pleased to meet you." To which Laurence, after winking at him, started to turn while telling him that she studied there every morning from Monday to Friday.

Schariar was bewildered by the direct attitude in which the woman conducted herself, and remained looking at Laurence until he felt a strong pull of his shirt. It was Ayesha, who surprised Schariar, since he had never before treated her like that.

"What's wrong?" he asked in a delicate tone.

"Nothing! Only that we're in a hurry to meet the general manager of the institute and you just had to stop and chat," Ayesha replied.

"Oh, so you're jealous!" Schariar grinned.

"Am not! You must be imagining things, that girl probably made you forget what we had planned," she said in a huff.

"Jealous, Ayesha is jealous!" Schariar chuckled.

She frowned and walked straight to the general manager's office. Upon arrival, they asked the secretary for Mr. Fernando Gómez; and after some questions and introductions, she took them into his office.

Upon entering, they noticed that in front of the desk a dark-skinned man was standing, he was of about forty years of age, overweight and with short hair. He asked them to come in and take a seat, and then asked them what was the reason for their visit. Ayesha explained the idea of the meeting of the Miraflores hotel general managers. Once she had finished speaking, Mr. Fernando explained that it was impossible for him to help them because he could not find a strong enough reason to justify that meeting of businessmen.

When Schariar heard the man give them his response, he jumped and exclaimed, "For God's sake, forgive me if I make a fool of myself for speaking out of turn but, Mr. Fernando, the reason for having a meeting with them is more than important. I don't know if you are aware that an exhibition of jewelry of the world will be held in a hotel in Miraflores?"

"So that was it!" replied the general manager. "And what about it?"

"That Mr. Fernando, as you can imagine, is a great temptation for a band of thieves and extortionists. And what we intend to do with that meeting is to find out in which hotel and on what date the jewelry exhibition is going to take place."

The manager was startled and with a loud voice said, "Good God, what do you intend to do with that jewelry display?"

Schariar laughed and then replied, "Nothing, how can you think that about us? Nevertheless, we know who will try to steal them."

"Tell the police," the businessman replied.

"That wouldn't work, because they do not have a clue about any of it and, indeed, they do not even know this band," Ayesha replied.

"But I cannot risk the lives of these people at the mere whim of two young people."

Schariar was feeling incredibly frustrated by the way the man was treating them, so he could not help but raising his voice, "Sir, we've warned you. If, as a consequence of one of the greatest jewel heists in Peru, which would amount to at least several million dollars, someone dies, it will only be your fault because you were able to help two people who had everything figured out better than the police and were about to catch the thieves, and you chose not to help!"

After he finished those words, he signaled Ayesha with his head and they both walked out of the office.

The manager was left disturbed and confused.

Schariar and Ayesha were already leaving the main office when the secretary called out to them, telling them that the manager was asking for them. Immediately they returned to Mr. Fernando's office.

When he saw them, the general manager rose and apologetically asked them to take a seat. They did and the three ended up agreeing that the meeting would be held in five days. Schariar tried to make it happen earlier; but Mr. Fernando explained that they had to put together the invitations, find the venue and organize the event, as well as taking care of many other details which made it impossible to carry out the event before. He also told them that the conference venue was already reserved for a four-day retreat. With nothing else to do, the young couple chose to retire and meet again one day before the meeting. They said good-bye and left the office.

Schariar and Ayesha felt happy, all the plans were progressing as they envisioned them and if they continued in that path, they would be able to hit Smith hard. They were talking while they walked through the halls of the institute when Schariar heard that someone was calling out his name. Turning to look who was calling him, he found himself facing Laurence's beautiful face who coyly invited him to walk up to his group so that she could introduce him to her friends. Ayesha was furious at the girl's move, but without giving away how mad she was the young woman went to sit on a bench by the door.

Laurence introduced Schariar to her four friends and invited him out on Saturday, February 7. Schariar pondered the possibility of the outing falling on the date of the exhibition, but after a while he accepted, saying to himself that if that happened he would have no choice but to apologize and postpone going out with his new friends to another day. After agreeing on the details of their date, he said goodbye to Laurence and her friends.

As he approached Ayesha, she leveled a very serious glare at him. To which Schariar explained that he wanted to have friends in this place and that maybe those girls could do them a favor when they needed it. He also explained that he had been invited to the cinema on February 7, and that he mentioned her, telling them that Ayesha would also go out with the group.

She calmed down a bit, but speaking loudly, she warned him not to forget the date of the jewelry exhibition and that they had to be there without fail.

The institute's guard, who was walking very close by, couldn't help but listen to their conversation. He was troubled by it and wondered what would the youngsters be doing involved in such an exhibition.

As the friends walked from the front door to the sidewalk the guard said to himself: "An exhibit of jewels! If I were still working in my previous profession, I'd surely be planning to steal them!" After a few minutes he forgot the subject and continued with his work as if nothing had happened.

After they left the institute, the young people took the first taxi that came along and went to their apartment. After a few minutes there, they went out to buy some food because they had decided to stay inside their residence until February 3, the day before the meeting of the main managers of Miraflores' hotels in CENFOTUR, date in which they'd decide all the details with Mr. Fernando.

The institute's guard, who was walking very close by, couldn't help but listen to their conversation. He was troubled by it and wondered what would the youngsters be doing involved in such an exhibition.

Everything Will Work Out, Smith!

Meanwhile, Fabian was meeting with his ten old companions, in an old quinta of the Barrios Altos of Lima. He was surprised by Joaquin's answer, a thin young man of about thirty-one, when he asked what became of Faustino Guerrero, his most faithful friend of the past. Joaquin had said that he had not heard from him for more than five years and that, as he had long ago learned, he had left the path of the underworld to devote himself to working honestly.

Fabian couldn't believe it, how was it possible that a former cohort of his would retire from this life of dark paths, it was something he could not understand. *Oh well*, he said to himself, *to each his own destiny*. And he decided to put the subject aside for the time being.

The eleven then divided into three groups to find out the whereabouts of the young people. The only thing they had, in terms of clues, was that they were two: One was a young man, with mustache and beard, of white complexion, and about 1.78 meters in height. The other was a girl, with about 1.76 meters in height, white complexion and big eyelashes. That, and that they were seen by them only once around the district of Miraflores. After sharing the information, each group went their own way to start the search.

Joaquín, Esteban, and Fabián decided to go meet Smith as he was going to share a plan he thought would be best to capture the young people and that assured them an 85% certainty in their quest.

When Smith learned of the way Fabian was conducting the search, he exclaimed, "Hallelujah, you finally are doing something right! But do not underestimate them... and know that I want them safe and sound. Do not fail me this time, because if you do you already know what will happen to you... Now go."

Once Fabian was out of Smith's sight, his comrade Joaquin reproached him by saying, "So you let yourself be beaten down by your boss! I think we should abandon him..."

"Who does he think he is? You do him a favor and see how he repays you," added Esteban.

"Shut up, idiots!" Fabian nearly shouted, exasperated by his friends' negativity. "He's the boss and I'd work with him even if it costs me my life! Only a select few get to join his crew."

Joaquin and Esteban looked at each other irked, but they had to resign themselves to pursuing the search without much detail.

Meanwhile in the hideout, Smith was giving directions to the most skillful investigator of his men. Gregory Bünge, who, with a typical German accent, only answered, "Yes, I understood!" Smith instructed him to watch the comings and goings of the hotel manager, Miguel Segura, and that any suspicious movement should be immediately reported to him by radio. It was a delicate job, but for Gregory it was child's play since it could not be compared to the difficult moments he had experienced when he was dealing narcotics. After receiving that order, he left the house and jumping on his motorcycle started to drive towards Miraflores.

The following order was for Edward Felix, expert in all types of firearms; Juan Lopez, expert in opening all kinds of locks; And Carlos Chuquihuanca, a soulless thief who specialized in escapes and riots. Smith told them that starting on the first of February, or the next day, they needed to be stationed in the district of Ancon, about a kilometer away from the Pasamayo highway.

"You'll take the truck, and you, Edward, will be responsible for returning it to me in good condition. According to reports I have received from Mario Cassimiro, the yacht that's coming with our gun shipment will arrive at about 11:30 p.m. on the first of February, about a kilometer from Pasamayo. Don't worry about the Ancon police, they've already been bribed. Although, you'll have to be careful not to tip off the army stationed at the docks. However, because they'll be changing their guard at that time, there will be a break in the watch, and we estimate that the exchange of merchandise should be quick enough to go unnoticed at that time. Now, I'm going to give you this briefcase containing the money needed for our order: a hundred rounds of machine gun bullets and about the same amount for handguns, twenty-five machine guns, two boxes of dynamite, two boxes of grenades, twenty-five automatic pistols, twenty-five silencers, ten rifles with telescopic and infrared eyes for the night, ten binoculars, fifteen bullet-proof vests and fifty field knives," Smith said.

After giving them the list of weapons they had to collect, he told them to go out and not return until they had everything in the order.

Before he left Edward exclaimed, "Well, with an

armament like that we could stage a coup d'etat!" And with a slight smile he said goodbye to them.

After the three of them left, Smith addressed Javier Lamp by saying, "And for you, for being the person I trust the most, I'm giving you the most important mission and you'll responsible for the fulfillment of the orders given to Edward, Juan and Carlos. Edward is a good man, but he is too confident in himself. He always thinks he can win and that is a detail that should be taken into account when working with him. But you, Javier, are more level-headed and intelligent; and, together with Gregory, I entrust you with the mission of taking care of the crew," he said, clasping his arm around his shoulders.

After Smith said those words, he gave Javier a cigar that he lit before he did his own. They both smoked and flooded the simple and dark environment with the smell.

"Smith, don't worry, I assure you, everything will be all right!" Javier said and left the lair to fulfill the mission.

An Unknown Security Guard

That night Schariar was in his apartment's living room watching the news, when he was stunned to hear more accurate details of the January 15 bank robbery near the University of San Marcos. At that moment, he shouted, "Ayesha, come listen to this!"

They reported that the six hooded individuals who robbed the bank were part of an international band wanted by the Interpol, the international police, and that they had nothing to do with any guerrilla group as it was believed in the beginning. They also said that their real names were not known.

"The police are following their tracks, but have no solid information yet. After the criminals left the bank, the employees showed the authorities an enigmatic clue left by the assailants. An "S" made up of twelve gold coins. The police believe that this is some sort of special symbol for the group. The amount of money stolen from the bank's own vaults in broad daylight amounts to $1,430,000, a sum that up to now had never been taken at any single robbery by any group. Police officials say that the gang arrived in our country not too long ago and suspect that they are here because of a jewelry exhibit to be held in a hotel in the capital. The representatives of the establishments involved are expected to take extensive security measures."

At the end of the news report, Schariar couldn't help but laugh.

"How can you laugh, they're dangerous criminals, they've killed people, and we're in the middle of all this!" Ayesha said in astonishment.

"Don't you see it?" Schariar exclaimed. "The cops don't know anything about the band, Interpol is searching for them without knowing their names; and yet we know almost all their movements, the names of those involved, the address of their new hiding place, and, moreover, the mystery that the police is trying to solve: the meaning of the S. There's no doubt, Ayesha, that we know more than the police. You see, two years ago Smith and Mario performed a great crime which they called "The eleven gold coins." Then came the robbery of that bank, which Smith called "The Twelve Coins of Gold." And the next robbery, which will become the greatest theft in Smith's career, stealing that jewelry, will be called "The Thirteen Gold Coins." As you can see, every crime he undertakes is marked with one more coin, what intrigues me is why would they form an S."

Amazed Ayesha kissed him on the cheek and exclaimed, "You're amazing, I'm certain we'll be able to bring down Smith and his gang!"

"Oh, don't fool yourself into thinking we're winning just yet, Ayesha, Smith is no idiot," Schariar said.

The day after seeing the news, the friends had breakfast and left to meet the general manager of CENFOTUR, it was already February 2nd and they needed to organize the meeting of executives.

As they arrived at CENFOTUR the young people entered the institute by the main door. They were lucky that at that moment the security guard was not at his post, otherwise he would have recognized them. When they entered, they went directly to the office of the general manager.

As they walked in the direction of the office, Ayesha murmured, "Please, don't let that girl show up now!"

"What girl are you talking about?" Schariar asked.

"Oh, nothing… I just remembered a classmate," Ayesha said, avoiding the conversation. Although she knew full well that it was difficult to hide something from her friend.

Upon entering the office of the general manager, he greeted them warmly and then explained that the meeting was organized without any setback and that the hotel managers invitations were made in absolute secrecy, assuring them that it would be almost impossible for outsiders to discover anything about the meeting.

When he heard the news, Schariar was happy and taking out a bundle of bills from his pocket, he replied, "Mr. Fernando, since the meeting will be held February 3rd at 7:30 at night, I am deeply grateful to you, and I will give you four thousand dollars to take care of the costs incurred, including those of the premises, food, snacks and related expenses as required."

Before leaving, the general manager addressed them saying, "Dear friends, if everything is as you're planning and we manage to capture these criminals, I would like to provide you with some scholarship or some important job in this institute, something to show my gratitude."

When Ayesha heard this she told the manager that they were content with being his friends in case they ever needed his help with something and that they didn't aspire to any particular job in the hotel industry. After saying this, they said goodbye to him and left the office.

Before arriving at the institute's exit, Schariar heard someone calling him. He had undoubtedly been discovered by Laurence.

Always known for his courtesy and humility, Schariar couldn't help but approach and talk to the beautiful girl. While this was happening, Ayesha exclaimed, "I was astonished not to see her when we came in!" She was upset, so she walked to the main door and left.

Seeing that Ayesha was leaving frustrated and without waiting for him, Schariar couldn't help but end the conversation and bid farewell to Laurence, since he definitely did not want to let his best friend leave by herself.

Meanwhile, Gregory Bünge was already getting impatient as he waited for the hotel manager to leave. As always, he was surveying the executive from a safe distance. Until that moment he had only followed him from the house to the hotel at 8:00 in the morning and vice versa at 5:00 in the afternoon, never anything different or that would alter his daily routine. Gregory was already on the edge of the exasperation because of the monotony of his work, when suddenly something startled him: it was already February 3rd, it was six o'clock in the afternoon, and the manager of the hotel was still inside.

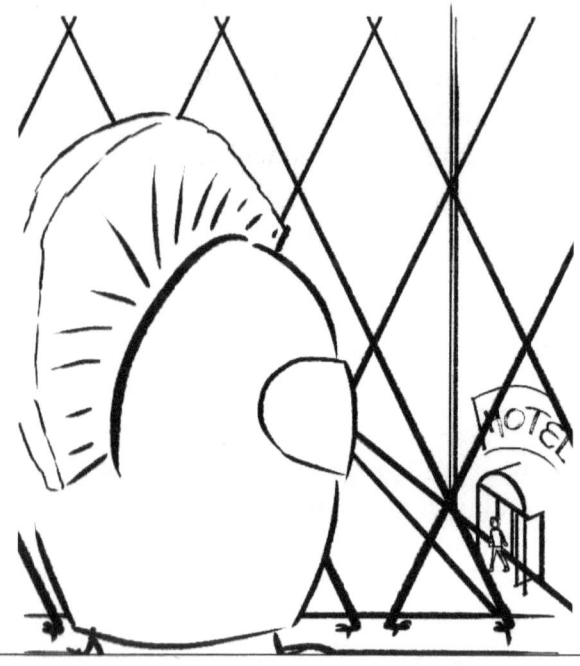

Meanwhile, Gregory Bünge was already getting impatient as he waited for the hotel manager to leave. As always, he was surveying from a safe distance.
At about 6:15 p.m. the manager left and got in his car; but instead of going home, he took another route in the direction of the Barranco district.

Bünge waited a little longer. At about 6:15 p.m. the manager left and got in his car; but instead of going home, he took another route in the direction of the Barranco district. Gregory stood on alert and followed him on his motorcycle at a safe distance. Then, about ten minutes away, the car stopped in front of a large house; there was a sign indicating that it was an institute of higher education. The manager got out of the car and entered the premises. From the appearance of the institute at that hour of the night Gregory assumed that some special meeting was being held inside.

Pretending to be a curious pedestrian, Gregory engaged in conversation with the doorkeeper. Through him he learned that the meeting was exclusively for representatives of hotels located in the city of Lima. In addition, he learned the name of the security guard, who in a moment of carelessness in the conversation let it slip that several years ago he had left behind his criminal career. After making such discoveries he said good-bye to the security guard as if they were good friends.

He immediately went to radio Smith and let him know about the latest intel. Upon learning of the meeting, Smith assumed that they were possibly discussing the final details of the exhibition that would be held on February 8; within five days.

After meditating on it for a while, Smith ordered Gregory to return to the house in La Molina.

That night, all the members of the gang gathered in the hiding place of La Molina to discuss the developments. Edward informed them that all the weapons were in good condition and that they did not suffered any mishap during the transaction. In addition, he gave Smith a letter sent by Mario through one of his messengers in the yacht. Smith read it silently:

February 12th
My friend Smith:

The weapons I've sent you as you know have a value of 1,000,000 dollars. I hope they are of good use to you, but do not forget our deal: 30% for me, the rest stays with you. As you can see, the amount is greater than previously agreed, but I do not object. I have great faith in you. Good luck.

Sincerely,
Mario Cassimiro

As he read the note, Smith could not help but find himself annoyed, exclaiming: "Mario always wants something extra!"

The members of the gang worried about the contents of the letter and the grimace of anger the boss made; but soon Smith settled himself and continued the conversation. And as he addressed Edward, he congratulated him for doing the job so well. Of course, he warned them, that this was only the beginning and that the difficult day of the exhibit was still to come. Then he went on to Charles.

"The next action item is yours. You've been chosen to take care of it because you are the one who knows thieves and outlaws in this city the best. I want you to go to the streets and bring me seven of the best; but be careful who you choose. I have great faith in you, do not fail me," Smith said.

After Carlos received the order, he left the house in search of his acquaintances. The rest of the group were amazed by this request, to the point that John said, "I don't understand what the boss wants with seven more people... Why? We can tackle this robbery alone!"

Hearing what John said, Smith stood up and calmly said, "So far the plan is working out and we are going to be successful, I will not fail you and I trust you will not either. On the day of the robbery you'll see why I planned it this way."

Right at that moment the door opened and Fabian came in to inform the boss that they were close to finding the young detectives because they had discovered that their address was somewhere in Avenida Pardo. Smith was pleased because he knew that with each day that passed he was closer to meeting those young people who had evaded his grasp for so long.

After learning all they had to know in preparation for the great jewelry theft, they all felt more relaxed and decided to go out and chill.

As they were leaving the hideout, Gregory started to talk with Fabian, and as they talked about their lives Gregory told him that when he was watching the hotel manager while at the tourist institute, he met the security guard; and what most caught his attention is that in one of his conversations he said, "Honest work is so much better than behaving like a street cat!"

When Fabian heard this he laughed and only managed to say, "Surely he's never been good at it."

Then Fabian, jokingly, asked if he knew his name by chance. Gregory laughed because the name of the security guard was the funniest to him, but after a while he said, "His name? He told me, it was... wait, I don't remember, it started with an F... I think I remember it: Ferepico... No, that's not it! Federico, yeah that's it, Federico Guerrero!" he shouted with joy as he remembered.

When he heard him say that name, Fabian almost fell on his face, he couldn't believe it. It was dumb luck Gregory found his old friend. And that made him very happy. So happy he even began to dance a little on the street. Gregory, Smith, and all the guys, were amazed and confused, and couldn't understand what had made Fabian so giddy. Until finally he calmed down enough to explain it to his comrades, "How can I not be happy, if I have found a brother with whom I had a covenant of blood and to whom I swore eternal loyalty? We promised that whatever happened to either of us, we'd be there for each other."

But Gregory interrupted him by saying, "Fabian, Federico works as a security guard and I do not think he wants to be a criminal again."

"It doesn't matter," Fabian said. "I won't ask him to come back, but a brother is a brother." After saying this, he stopped talking and continued dancing. After half an hour everyone retired to rest.

The Big Meeting

It was the afternoon of February 3rd, in the apartment of Avenida Pardo Ayesha and Schariar were getting ready to go to the institute, where the meeting with the hotel managers was about to take place.

Ayesha was wearing a beautiful blue dress; and when it was hit by artificial light, it sparkled like a diamond. She had a beautiful necklace and earrings of natural pearls and wore a pair of high-heeled patent leather shoes. Seeing her dressed in this way Schariar whistled at her and said, "Ayesha, you look like a princess! No, you are a princess." He wore a freshly pressed black suit made of English wool and black dress shoes.

They both truly looked like European royalty.

To complete the look, at the request of Ayesha and counting with the fabulous amount of one hundred thousand dollars that came from Smith's briefcase, Schariar bought a black Trans Am, latest model, with tinted windows. At night it looked like a fantastic car.

Before leaving the apartment, Schariar offered his arm to his partner and then they drove together to the meeting. When they arrived at the institute, the doorman opened the door and led them into the living room, but before entering, Schariar's gaze met the guard's. This did not please him, but he pretended as if it had not taken place.

Once inside, they met with Mr. Fernando, who

introduced them to all the representatives of the most distinguished hotels in the city of Miraflores.

After being introduced to everyone and exchanging a few words with them, Schariar moved on to the buffet table. Upon seeing him do this, Ayesha got upset. "How can you eat right now, when we're supposed to find the person in charge of the hotel!" she scolded her friend.

"Ayesha, you know I'm a hungry guy and I can't think on an empty stomach. Besides, the sandwiches look delicious," Schariar exclaimed. "Look, there's apple pie, strawberry, chocolates, sandwiches of all tastes, turkey, suckling pig, wines, spirits of all kinds and much more. How do you expect me to see this table and not get extremely hungry?"

When she heard this, Ayesha only said, "These men, all they see is food!" But a little while later she was enjoying the buffet too.

Once they were satisfied, and after finishing their conversation and completing their plan to find out the hotel where the exhibition would be held, they called Mr. Fernando and explained that Schariar wanted to speak to all the representatives. The general manager immediately managed to attract the attention of the public, and after the presentations and protocol he gave the spotlight to Schariar, who addressed them.

Once they were satisfied, and after finishing their conversation and completing their plan to find out the hotel where the exhibition would be held, they called Mr. Fernando and explained that Schariar wanted to speak to all the representatives.

"Good evening, Mr. Director of the study center, Mr. Manager and worthy representatives of the most respected hotels in Miraflores: I know the effort that you all put in to move forward the local, national and international tourism of our beloved Peru. For this reason, each one of you puts together conferences, exhibitions, competitions, tours and endless things to attract tourists. But, there are certain implacable enemies that destroy the desire for growth within us. These enemies are crime, drug trafficking, terrorism, inflation and excessive bureaucracy that exist in our country. Because of this, we have organized this meeting, to fight one of those evils."

Schariar paused as the audience clapped.

"There is a hotel, a worthy hotel, or rather, one that strives to attract those tourists. And, well, it does attract great variety of tourists: rich people, aristocrats, governors, oil executives and many more. These people bring to our country fresh foreign currency and much confidence for our entrepreneurs. The hotel that attract all these people has planned an exhibit, an exhibit like you've never seen in our country. It'll be the first exhibition of the most famous jewels in the world. And now I would like to ask the representative of that hotel to approach the office of the general manager of this institute. That's all I have to say, thank you very much for your attention."

At the end of Schariar's speech everyone applauded effusively, congratulating him on what he had said, saying that he had good oratorical attributes. He just thanked everyone and, taking Ayesha, they walked towards the administrative office to meet the hotel manager.

When they got there, they found Mr. Fernando and another man of advanced age. The manager introduced him as Miguel Segura, general manager of the hotel located at Avenida 28 de Julio 563 Miraflores, the place where the exhibition would be held on February 8.

When he learned this was the person he was looking for, Schariar thanked Mr. Fernando and the hotel manager for the valuable information and continued, "First of all, I want to congratulate the manager on coming to the office faster than we did."

"I came quickly because I was curious as to what you wanted to talk about," the manager replied.

"You must know, Mr. Segura, that your exhibit is threatened with robbery," Schariar explained.

"I cannot believe it!" the manager exclaimed.

"Yes, Mr. Segura, as I said, threatened by an international criminal enterprise band. The police know almost nothing about them, but we know almost all their movements."

"But you did warn the police, the army, or whoever is best, to catch them, correct?" the hotel manager interrupted.

"That's not possible, it would ruin our whole plan," Schariar said. "In due time we will alert them, but for now we need you to do as we say, Mr. Segura: hide the real jewels somewhere, somewhere no one would suspect, and replace them with fakes. These must be an exact replica of the original ones. They should be kept where the true jewels are kept now and exhibited during the day to the public. Never, in any circumstance, take out the legitimate ones."

"But if one of the customers wants to buy, we cannot hand them the fake ones. It would mean to deceive them and throw away the hotel's prestige," interrupted the manager.

"Oh, don't worry about that!" Schariar said. "You know how to treat the public by telling them that they will send the jewelry to their respective address when the exhibition ends. I do not think the customer will be suspicious if the hotel wishes to exhibit them a bit longer, don't you think, Mr. Segura?"

"Oh yes, yes of course!" replied the manager.

"Then we'll tell the police to be alert day and night, but they must be dressed in civilian clothes. In the streets we will place about ten agents, stationed around the hotel and even on the roofs of the surrounding buildings; and inside the hotel, especially in the exhibition hall, about five agents in each setting pretending to be part of the public. Do you understand Mr. Segura?"

"Yes, of course!" the manager replied.

"Well, do everything I told you, we'll take care of the rest. Now, where we can we find you if we need to talk?" Schariar replied.

"At my office in the hotel, on the fifth floor, just ask for the manager Segura and say it's from you."

After everything was ready, the friends said good-bye and left the office. But before doing so, Schariar decided to go to the buffet table to bring something to eat on the way home.

"Schariar, how much are you going to eat? You're going to become a pig!" Ayesha exclaimed.

"Come on, Ayesha, are you going to start with that again? I think you should also eat something. Let me tell you: I feel like every sandwich or dessert I eat will cost me hundreds of dollars and I can't stop feeling pleasure from eating one more."

"Of course!" Ayesha replied. "The buffet and the decorations have cost us a bundle."

"Oh my God, I forgot about that!" Schariar said while faking distress.

Both started to laugh while walking to the entrance, then got in the car and left. As they headed for Avenida Pardo, Schariar could not help but feel pleasure to be driving such an outstanding car, he even had certain air of pride.

Ayesha realized the change in the attitude of Schariar and decided to say something. "You know that vanity and haughtiness are only valued by frivolous and despicable people?"

"Oh! Yes I know, Ayesha, and I'm not haughty, but I like this car and I think you should also buy one that you like. Anyway, it's good to indulge yourself from time to time... don't you think?"

"It's possible you're right, Schariar. Maybe after we're done with this case I'll buy a car that I like," she replied.

I forgot to tell you that Schariar's car had tinted windows to keep people from seeing him; or if in the future he became more involved in the world of crime, his enemies could not recognize him. He was also planning to turn his Trans Am into an armored car in the future, but without damaging the original frame of the car.

Old Friends Encounter

Fabian woke up the next day with the idea of looking up his old buddy, so he asked Gregory for the address of the institute where he worked and hurried to leave.

At about 2:30 in the afternoon the CENFOTUR security guard spotted at about seventy meters from the door an individual walking towards him. His style of walking reminded him of an old friend of his. And when he had the man in front of him, he was astonished; he couldn't believe that his friend really was there!

When they met, they hugged each other tightly and began to talk about everything that had happened to them in the last six years, since they went their separate ways. Fabian was amazed and perhaps a little amused to see him dressed in a security guard uniform, and it felt strange to hear Federico talking about leaving behind the world of crime.

Federico asked him what was he doing currently and Fabian, recognizing that he couldn't avoid the question since years ago the two always agreed to be honest with one another, he answered that at that moment he belonged to Smith's gang of thieves, and that they were looking for clues and making plans to steal some jewelry which would be displayed in a hotel in Miraflores.

Federico was taken aback by the news and Fabian

asked him why did he have that reaction.

"Oh, I just remembered something," Federico replied. "About five days ago, I saw a couple of young people coming out of here, and the girl was shouting at the boy, "Do not forget that we have to be at the jewelry exhibition that day!" The strange thing is that I assume that exhibition is for adults that belong to a certain aristocratic high class and not for two young people like them."

When he heard what his friend was saying, Fabian had to take a seat because he almost fainted in light of the news. After reacting, Fabian could not stop thanking Federico for the information. He did not know why he thanked him and asked, "Why are you thanking me for? What did I say? Are you interested in those youngsters?"

"Of course!" cried Fabian, "I've been looking for them for days and I still haven't found them. Those kids want to ruin our plans and I need to catch them, our boss wants to meet them."

When he heard what he was saying, Federico could not but murmur, "That's what those two were afraid of, I see it now! And if you were a stranger, I wouldn't tell you what I'm going to tell you, but, having a pact with you and as a brother, I'll inform you of the following: You'll know that you can catch the young people on February 7, because that day they will have a date with a group of girls from the institute at 5:30 p.m., according to what I heard a few days ago when they came and the young man engaged in a conversation with a student. But, yes, you will have to get them away from here so that the heads of the institute do not know and I'm not forced to report the crime."

When Fabian learned of the news and listened to Federico's recommendations, he swore to do it in such a way that neither he nor anyone else would know about the kidnapping.

Federico then informed him that the two friends were driving a black Trans Am with tinted windows.

After Federico told Fabian everything he knew, Fabian thanked him for the good news and for saving him, because his life depended on it, and then they continued talking for half an hour about other trivial subjects until he had to leave. To Fabian the most astonishing thing was that everything was due to a chance encounter between Gregory and Federico.

Upon arriving at La Molina's hideout and informing Smith of the news, the boss felt relaxed and congratulated him while mumbling, "At last I'll be able to meet them and have the pleasure of being able to carry out the plan smoothly while those youngsters are in my hands."

Last Details

It was February 6th, two days before the big business meeting at the institute. Schariar and Ayesha got in the car and left from the Avenida Pardo apartment toward the hotel, they were going to meet with the manager for the last time to take care of the final details of the exhibition. Upon arrival at the hotel they asked at reception for Segura the manager, and after giving their names they were welcomed and quickly escorted to the manager's office.

Once they were alone with the manager, he informed them that everything had been arranged in accordance with the plan and that the real jewels were stored in a safe in a bank in the city and that no one but his wife knew where they were. And just as planned, the fake ones took the place of the originals. Twenty private guards and twenty police officers in civilian clothes were also hired; and they would provide surveillance inside and outside the hotel.

He invited them to the hall where the exhibition was going to be held. This was a rather large room, divided into several smaller rooms, and everything was exquisitely decorated; pictures of famous painters with gold leaf on the frame edges, fine curtains and carpets brought from the Middle East. The false jewels were so well made that the most knowledgeable person would have difficulty recognizing. They were located in their respective showcases. Each one was distanced by a space of 1.50 meters, allowing the flow of the public without difficulty. It seemed to Schariar that everything was organized as they agreed. So it would be almost impossible for a group to enter and take the jewels without notice, but since this was Smith's crew he felt it wasn't a good idea to underestimate him. He also recommended monitoring the hotel vaults.

Everything was ready to go for the big day. After showing them the room, the manager invited them to have lunch at the hotel. Schariar ordered a dish he had never tasted, a filet mignon with some kind of red wine sauce served with golden potatoes, he definitely was very curious to find out how did he liked that dish. Ayesha chose not to try her luck and ordered her favorite, a simple lasagna with meat sauce, and the manager ordered a poor-style rib-eye steak with French fries.

They talked for a long time and joked as they dined as friends. After saying goodbye, they returned to the apartment, arriving late at night. They were so tired that once they entered Schariar's place they laid down in bed and fell asleep soundly.

Meanwhile, Fabian joined the group of ten to inform them of the news regarding the two young friends, he told them that they would no longer have to keep looking for them because he had found them and told them about his encounter with Federico. The only thing left for them to do was to be at the CENFOTUR Institute at 5:15 p.m. on February 7th, fifteen minutes before the time when the two youngsters would arrive to meet with a group of friends to go that night to the movies.

"We will follow them until the movie ends and once their friends leave them by themselves we will follow them home and kidnap them before they make it inside. That way, we will avoid being seen by anybody and we'll also know where the two live, in case we need to go back some time later. After that, we will take them to meet Smith. Of course, be warned, watch your manners. Smith wants them safe and sound, without a scratch, otherwise we'll pay with our skin."

His crewmembers swore to behave around the young folks. However, one of them, named Peter, grumbled and said, "Oh, Fabian, you know very well how attracted I am to women, if she is very beautiful I do not think I can stop my urges!"

To which Fabian replied, "It may cost you your life if you don't keep it to yourself. If Smith finds out you lay a single finger on the girl, you'll be the little fish's breakfast and I'll be her lunch."

"Oh, shut up already... and... okay, I'll behave!" grudgingly muttered Peter.

Without suspecting anything, and while they were driving to the movie theater, they didn't notice that a dark van with four people on board was following them.

Because of a Date

Schariar and Ayesha got ready to meet with Laurence and her friends. They agreed to meet at the institute on February 7 at five in the afternoon and then go for a drive or to a movie.

They got into the car and headed towards the place. On their way to the date, they both agreed they would not stay past midnight or at most one o'clock in the morning so they could be fresh on the day of the exhibition and react at the precise moment of the robbery.

When they arrived at the institute they saw that the girls were already waiting for them. Laurence greeted Schariar and Ayesha by introducing them to her friends.

Everyone got in the car. Ayesha, Schariar, and Laurence sat in the front and the other four girls in the back. As they talked and planned what movies to go see, they did not cease to lavish praise and admiration for the Trans Am, and to ask him how he could afford it.

"A guy gave it to me!" he answered. He did not dare to tell them the truth, otherwise he could have been involved in serious problems.

Without suspecting anything, and while they were driving to the movie theater, they didn't notice that a dark van with four people on board was following them.

They talked so much in the car that time flew by

and when they finally arrived at the cinema they had closed the sale of tickets for the movie they wanted to see, so they decided to change their destination and go to Boulevard San Ramón, better known as "pizza street," located in the heart of Miraflores, to eat something light and drink *sangría*.

Meanwhile, in the van with the tinted windows that had been following them all night, the occupants were surprised to see that instead of going to the movies they went to a pizza shop. They had no choice but to park the car at a safe distance from the Trans Am and then walk to a place close to where the young people were toasting. They asked for a couple of pitchers of *sangría* to make time and managed to watch them without being suspicious.

It was about 1:30 in the morning when Schariar and his friends decided to call it a night. They got in the car and Schariar drove each of them to their homes. Luckily, they all lived relatively close by, between the city of Miraflores and Barranco; except Laurence, who resided in Chaclacayo. Seeing that it would be too much for them to go all the way there as late as it was, Schariar invited her to spend the night in his apartment.

Laurence had no problem with the plan, but Ayesha frowned without giving any opinion, even though it would have been unfair to leave her alone in the street to take a taxi as it was undoubtedly dangerous.

After dropping off everyone else, and when they were about fifteen meters away from Schariar's building, all of a sudden they were ambushed by about ten armed people who easily transferred them to the truck and immediately headed to La Molina.

Among the three, Laurence was the most frightened because she had no idea why they were being abducted. Although they lived in a time of constant muggings and kidnappings, they were not on the list of wealthy people that could interest the mafias.

Schariar remained quiet and calm, he didn't utter a word throughout the journey; but Ayesha kept asking loudly why they were being kidnapped and where were they taking them.

"Who are you? Why are you doing this? Who's your boss?" Ayesha waited for a reply from them, and when she saw that they weren't going to respond, she insisted again, "What's wrong with you? Are you deaf? Answer me!"

After a while, the one who appeared to be the leader turned toward her and replied, "Don't be impatient, you're going to meet our boss, he's anxious to see you." After that he didn't say a word until they reached the hideout.

As they made them get out of the car very kindly, Pedro, another of the kidnappers, tried to touch Laurence, but at that moment he felt Fabian's hand on his shoulder as he reminded him, "You'll become the fish's breakfast, remember? Leave her alone."

Schariar looked unruffled during the journey, but before entering the thieves den he murmured into Ayesha's ear, "I think I know who wants to meet us and apparently he doesn't want us dead."

"That's what I think too," Ayesha replied, and

continued, "But what about Laurence? She's scared and knows nothing."

"Don't worry, Laurence is strong," he said. "Don't you agree, Laurence?

"I think so, but I'd like you to explain," Laurence replied.

They were taken to a large space. They saw several cars parked around and a big table in the center with about twenty chairs.

"Boss!" cried Fabian. "I bring you the young people you longed to meet, the would-be detectives. It was a lot of work but at last we finally caught up with them."

At that moment Smith got up from his chair, had the young friends untied and invited them to sit down. Amazed, Fabian exclaimed, "But boss, they'll escape!"

"Don't be afraid," Smith said, "These young people are smart enough not to even think about it." And as he winked at Schariar, he asked, "Am I right my young detective?"

Schariar didn't answer but rather sat down quietly.

Smith began the interrogation.

"I was anxious to meet you, I've seen that your cunning and intelligence is greater than that of the agents of the national police. I imagine you are newcomers to this type of task, but with all the tricks and traps you have played on me and being that this is the first time in my life that some strangers have gotten so close to putting me in hot water, you have achieved the honor of having my deepest respect. If it had been any other person, it would have been enough for me to eliminate it, but I don't want it to be that way... I just want to get you out of my way."

Smith paused to take a breath and asked, "What are your names?"

"Schariar and Ayesha, the young detectives!" the young man replied.

Smith looked at them carefully, and after hearing their names as he flooded the room with a puff of smoke from the cigar in his mouth, he went on, "You want to know something? From the day you left me that first letter, and then the rest of things that happened with such acuity and audacity, I knew that I was not in front of some simple private investigators, that's why I can forgive the things you've done, like taking my money. Of course, I will hold you captive here so that you won't be in the way any longer. Tomorrow is our day and nobody will stop us. In addition, I will leave you a small gift if case you manage to escape because in less than twenty-four hours this whole house will blow up."

Smith took a bundle of ten thousand dollars from the recovered bag and went on, "If you can escape you can take this money. I've never been so magnanimous with people who have caused me so much trouble."

He exhaled another puff of smoke and, more relaxed, he continued, "You'll have two options, to die or to live with something extra."

At that moment Schariar replied, "I agree, but let Laurence and Ayesha go! They can't die like this, they're beautiful women with their whole futures ahead of them."

"I'm sorry, young man, my sentence has been given. Now I'm going to rest... and have a good night in your chambers," Smith said and walked away laughing.

Javier Lamp and Fabian took the three young people to the adjoining room. They tied their feet and hands in such a way they were forced to sleep in a seated position, back to back, and unable to move their feet or arms. They also gagged them so that they could not speak either. Before leaving them alone in the room they checked that they didn't have any weapon or something similar to it. But as luck would have it, Schariar always carried a small knife hidden inside the shoe in a small secret pocket next to the laces, which prevented it from being discovered.

Once they thought they had everything under control they entered the main hall to loot the jewelry cases, but at that moment they felt six shots in the air and an order, "Hands up, you're under arrest!"

Double Punch

February 8th arrived. Inside the hotel a tense and hectic environment set the tone as preparations for the big event were underway and the employees worked hard on the last details for the great exhibition of world famous jewels. The security staff took the maximum precautions for any kind of risk, and was on high alert as they patrolled among the guests and general public.

It was eight o'clock at night, at that time the exhibition was at its peak attendance. Meanwhile, seven individuals were moving in the dark along the left-hand side of the hotel, knocking down four private security guards and entering through the driveway to the basement, up from the cargo elevator to the seventh floor, where the event was taking place. When they got out of the elevator, the first thing they did was fire a machine gun into the air and immediately gave orders that everyone present laid on the ground, not realizing that five police officers had hidden behind a counter that stood close to the path the assailants were going to use to move around.

Once they thought they had everything under control they entered the main hall to loot the jewelry cases, but at that moment they felt six shots in the air and an order, "Hands up, you're under arrest!"

One of the assailants suddenly spun with the intention of firing, but he was shot in the abdomen and immediately fell to the ground. The agents then went on to handcuff all the men, taking them out and putting them at the disposal of the "black eagle squadron", a police squadron specialized in kidnapping and terrorist acts. Once in the patrol, they were taken to the police headquarters.

While this was happening, the hotel manager was deeply concerned because he couldn't find Schariar or Ayesha. They were supposed to meet him at the exhibit at six in the afternoon, and it was already ten o'clock at night. And they had not called him on the phone or answered his calls.

For a minute the manager hesitated about the young detectives, he even thought they might be part of the band; but, after a moment of reflection, he said to himself: *No! They can't be. Besides, if it were not for these young friends, they would have taken all the jewels away. How could I think ill of them, it could be that they're in trouble, but how to help them?*

That same day, at Smith's hiding place in La Molina, everyone was preparing for the big scene to be held at 4:30 am, because at that time the place would be quiet and with all the public already retired they would only have to disarm a few custodians.

Going back to the hotel...

Seeing that it was already 3:40 a.m. and almost all the general public had retired, the general manager decided to end the exhibition and store the jewelry in the vault located on the same floor, in an adjoining room, and towards the wall facing the back window. After storing all the jewels in a safe place, he thought that no more security agents would be necessary, because the seven men had already been arrested that night, so he sent half of them home. This was a horrible mistake that would be noticed too late.

The streets of Miraflores at that hour were silent waiting for the sunrise, and the atmosphere was quite cold and humid due to the persistent drizzle of the winter season, the only living creatures that were observed out there were the security agents at the hotel.

4:15 a.m., five of the ten agents went to buy some cigarettes; they walked to the only place that worked at that time, about thirty meters away from the hotel on the opposite sidewalk. Meanwhile, on the other side, the remaining five unarmed agents were ambushed and quickly knocked unconscious by Smith's crew. Then they dressed quickly in their victims' uniforms and entered the hotel quietly, as part of the round of security at that time. They reached the seventh floor without any mishap and as soon as they stepped into the room they whacked the four guards inside, forcing them to give them the key to the safe at the cost of their lives.

Once the key was obtained, it was easy for them to open the vault and put all the jewels in their bags. Then they tied up the guards and left them inside the safe, but without closing the door. It was a merciful act of the boss, for it was not his intention to let them suffocate to death.

When they were done, they took the corridor that led to the emergency staircase behind the building, and there's where they had a setback as they faced off with four security agents; but after a short conversation and a few accurate blows they got rid of them and continued going down until they arrived at the roof of a neighboring house adjoining the hotel. From there they went from rooftop to rooftop to the other street. *The plan was perfect*, Smith thought as he approached the van through a dark corridor, and said to himself, *When the people at the hotel realize that the jewels have been stolen we will be far away.*

At the exact moment of opening the door of the truck, intent on leaving, a person with a gun in his hand came out of the car, it was one of the many policeman surrounding them. Smith and all his group were petrified, allowing themselves to be arrested without even putting up resistance.

Before being taken to the police headquarters, Smith asked the captain of the police squad, "How did you know we were here? I can't believe this happened, our plan was perfect! How did you do it?"

The lieutenant in command of the operation approached Smith to answer, "It's all thanks to some young detectives." He pointed his finger at a corner of the wall. "Schariar and Ayesha, you can come out now!"

"I've should've known," Smith mumbled.

The Final Scene

Before getting in the patrol car to be taken to the police headquarters and from there to the courthouse, Smith gave the boys a glance as he said, "I congratulate you for the good work you've done, we will meet again someday."

"I think so too, Smith," Schariar said, and continued, "I wish you good luck with your jewels, as fake as they are, and thank you for the money, your house in La Molina was destroyed, hopefully you can rebuild it.

Smith, upon hearing what Schariar had to say about the jewels, looked at him deeply, and with reckless respect murmured, "I hope you're lucky on the next one. By the way: those bills are not real either," he said as he closed the window and the police patrol car set off for the police headquarters.

Schariar and Ayesha said farewell to all who participated in the capture, and as they drove to Chaclacayo to take Laurence home, the young man explained how they, the young detectives, got involved in that case and became the main promoters of the plan to trap those thieves red-handed.

After leaving Laurence speechless and safe at home, Schariar and Ayesha drove back to the apartment at Avenida Pardo in Miraflores to rest, because they were exhausted after everything that happened.

Meanwhile, the patrol car that took Smith and his group to the police headquarters in Lima reached its destination. The cops escorted him through the main door of the building and then headed up the stairs to the third floor. After climbing a few steps, Smith threw himself on the floor, and in a state of panic asked them to take him in the elevator; he explained that he had seizures because every time he climbed the stairs and looked down, the slits on the steps reminded him of past traumas that he had not been able to overcome. So loud was his plea and great his history of his psychological hang-ups that he managed to persuade them to accept his request.

Already in the elevator, and almost reaching the second floor, Smith, in a swift motion, turned the lights off, and then there was a knock and a jerk. When the elevator arrived on the seventh floor and the doors opened, the officers realized that they had hit another of the assailants, and two people were missing: the leader of the band and one of his assistants. The guards didn't know what to do or how to explain to their chief the escape of these two individuals within the police headquarters.

Hours later they managed to discover that they escaped through the roof of the elevator, climbing up one of the cables to the roof and then climbing down to the street by one of the unused electric cables stored in a box on the roof. By that time Smith and his inseparable bodyguard, Javier Lamp, must have surely been quietly and freely walking the quaint streets of downtown Lima.

The next morning, after washing quickly and eating a frugal breakfast, Schariar turned on the television to find out if the theft of jewels they had managed to stop was in the news. The noise he caused woke up her friend who was still enjoying a deep sleep.

"TVNews Lima, channel 7 reports: Yesterday at 7 in the morning two individuals suspected of the failed jewelry theft in a hotel in Miraflores mysteriously escaped from the city police headquarters without leaving any trace. According to the latest investigation, they would have done so by climbing the elevator cables and then reaching the roof from where the suspects would have got down to the streets using ropes. The police have already given the alert and offered a reward for help in their capture. They are considered two dangerous offenders of international fame. If someone has valuable information about these escaped individuals, please call the police telephone number on the screen, your call will be kept in anonymity."

Schariar looked at Ayesha as he said, "Our esteemed rival, Smith, is free, and I think very soon we will receive an invitation from the police to help them. What new adventures will destiny have for us?"

"I do not know, my friend," she replied, and continued, "I don't like this at all. But we'll have to follow the path that destiny has prepared us." And after saying this she got up to eat her breakfast too…

Table of contents